W9-BIA-222

THE ISLAND OF THE SKOG

ANTIQUES
Remember to hug a RODENT on National Rodent Day
ROWDY CAPTAIN
THE FLYING ROSE
CAPE OF GOOD HOPE
LIVERPOOL · BATH · DUBLIN
HACKENSACK · NAPLES
"The Flying Rose"
A seaworthy ship model.

THE ISLAND OF THE SKOG

story and pictures by

STEVEN KELLOGG

Dial Books for Young Readers
New York

Library of Congress catalog card number: 73-6019
First Pied Piper Printing 1976
Printed in U.S.A.
(b)
12 14 15 13
A Pied Piper Book is a registered trademark of
Dial Books for Young Readers, a division of NAL Penguin Inc.
® TM 1,163,686 and ® TM 1,054,312
THE ISLAND OF THE SKOG is published in a hardcover edition by
Dial Books for Young Readers, 2 Park Avenue,
New York, New York 10016
ISBN 0-8037-4122-7

It was National Rodent Day, and Jenny decided to have a party. Hannah, Wooster, and Louise came. So did Bouncer and his buddies from the bowling alley.

They all arrived shaking after a narrow escape from the butcher's cat. Jenny decided to wheel in the dessert right away.

"Hot marshmallow cheese cake with raspberry fudge sauce!" she announced.

Meanwhile the cat had slipped in with the delivery boy. The mice just barely escaped to the basement.

"A German Shepherd got Granny last night," puffed Hannah. "We should stay in our own holes!"

"I'm tired of living in a hole," said Jenny.

"Let's fight for freedom!" cried Bouncer. "We'll be soldiers! Rough-riding Rowdies! I'll be the general and commander-in-chief!"

"Wait!" cried Jenny. "Let's sail away instead. We'll find a peaceful island."

The mice cheered.

"I'll be the ship's captain!" declared Bouncer. "Rowdies, you're my crew!"

It took the mice most of the night to load the ship and roll it to the harbor.

Ignoring the crowd at the pier, they sailed bravely out to sea.

During the first few days of the voyage the mice feasted on chocolate waffles and coconut cherry cheese pie. Between meals they dreamed of their island and tanned their pelts in the sun.

THE ROWDIES
RODENT LEAGUE
BOWLING CHAMPS
1973
1967
1963
IN PURSUIT OF HAPPINESS!
TRUTH
JUSTICE
EQUALITY
LIBERTY
LAW
BROTHERHOOD
PEACE
LOVE
FUN
YO HOHO
TWELVE CANNONBALLS FOR CANNONS OR BOWLING
MARCH 12
DEAR BABS
WE ARE HAVING FUN.
LOVE
HANNAH AND ME
ROBINSON
GEOGRAPHY

As the days passed, it grew colder and colder. The mice were unprepared for winter weather, and they huddled close to the waffle iron.

"Land ho!" cried Captain Bouncer one morning as the ship narrowly missed hitting an iceberg. The mice looked at the compass and discovered that they had been sailing toward the North Pole.

"The compass must've been upside down!" insisted Bouncer. "I'm tired of being captain anyway. I quit!"

By the time they reached warmer seas, their food supplies were very low. The mice were seasick, homesick, and convinced they would soon be dead.

"I'd give a billion dollars for one last chocolate-coated cheese puff," moaned a Rowdy.

Suddenly Jenny cried: "Land ho!"

"The book calls it the Island of the Skog," said Wooster. "It says: 'Population: One Skog.' But it doesn't say what a Skog is."

"If there's only one, then there's plenty of room for all of us," said Louise. "Why don't we bring it a gift so it will know we're friendly?"

"Wait a minute, flubberhead," snapped Bouncer. "Suppose this Skog is dangerous? Let's blaze our way to the island and show him we mean business!"

The Rowdies fired all twelve cannonballs, and then the mice waded cautiously ashore.

"I claim this land," cried Bouncer, "as a place where all mice can live without fear. We will build a great kingdom dedicated to the freedom of mice, and I will be the king!"

There were murmurs of surprise from the other mice.

"Here we can all *feel* like kings," said Jenny. "And that is the most important part of being king, as everyone knows."

After unloading their supplies, they somersaulted on the beach through the long, brilliant sunset. How wonderful it was to be on land again.

Finally, as the last rays of daylight faded, they climbed back aboard the ship to spend the night.

At dawn they discovered an enormous footprint in the sand.

"It looks like a bear track," said Hannah.

"Stand aside, tenderfeet," ordered Bouncer. "This is a job for the Rough-riding Rowdies! We'll use my grandpap's favorite trick. First dig a deep hole, then cover it with straw, and bait it with honey. Tonight the beast will smell the bait, stumble into the trap, and the island will be ours!"

By evening the trap was completed. The mice spent a sleepless night in a nearby hole.

The next morning they discovered that the trap was empty. "Look!" shrieked Hannah. "Someone cut the rope. The ship is gone."

"We're MAROONED!" wailed the mice.

"Our only chance now," said Bouncer, "is to get rid of the Skog before he gets rid of us. Who will volunteer?"

"It looks like a job for the Rough-riding Rowdies," said Jenny.

"Whose idea was it to come here anyway?" grumbled Bouncer.

All eyes turned back to Jenny.

"I have a plan," she said. "We must build a giant kite and tie it to a very long rope. We'll circle a honey jar with one end of the rope, and when the Skog steps into the circle, we will send the kite aloft. The Skog will be pulled into the air and towed out to sea."

That night the mice hid behind a sand dune and kept watch over the honey jar. Just after dawn a shadowy figure appeared on the beach.

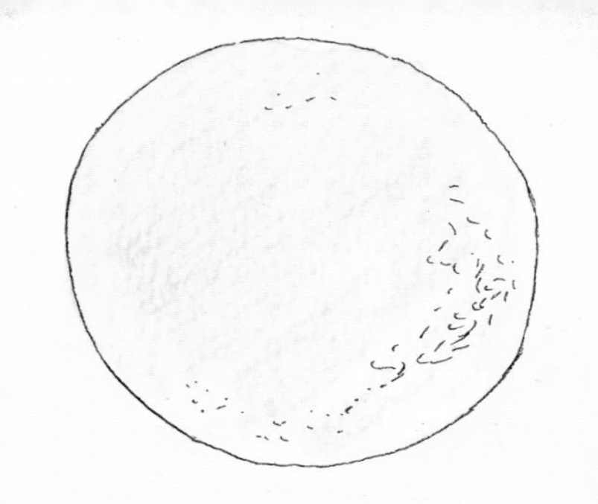

The monstrous creature lurched toward the honey jar. Trembling, the mice sent their kite high into the ocean wind.

HONEY
YOU'LL LOVE IT!!!

The plan had worked! But suddenly the Skog came flapping apart, and half of him plunged back to the island.

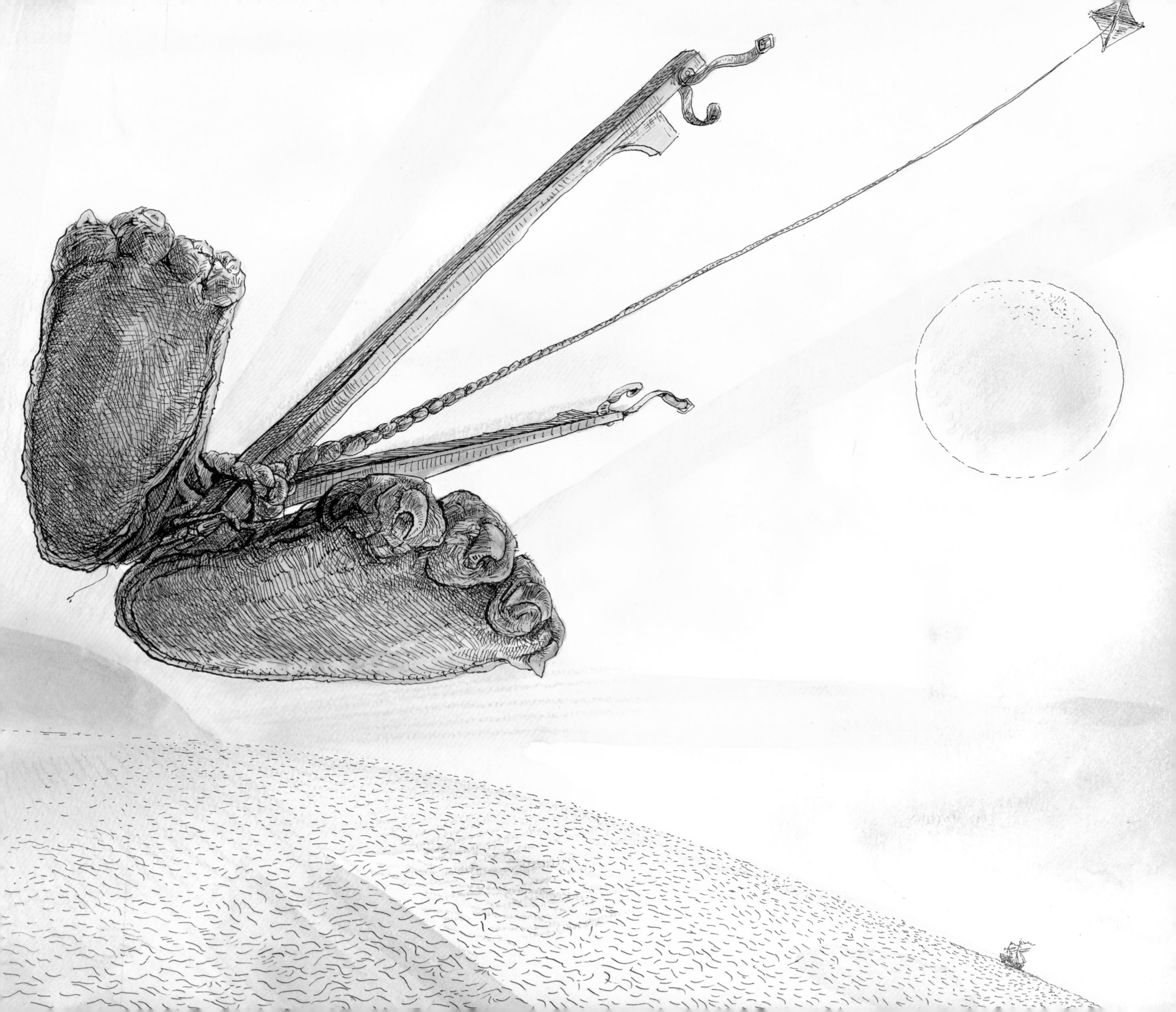

The fallen Skog lay flat and still.

"Surrender, you pirate!" puffed Bouncer.

Suddenly a little animal appeared. "Don't hurt me!" he cried.

"We won't hurt you," said Wooster. "We were afraid of you! Why did you wear this monster costume?"

"Because I was afraid of you!" cried the Skog. "I was frightened by your cannons and your trap!"

"What happened to our ship?" demanded Bouncer.

"I cut the rope because I thought you were sleeping on board," confessed the Skog. "I've been so lonely here, but I decided it was better to be alone than to be afraid."

"If only we'd talked to each other," said Jenny.

Bouncer stepped forward and helped the Skog to his feet.

They all agreed to build a village and live together.

"Let's make plans right now!" suggested Bouncer. "The first thing we'll need is a national anthem. Rowdies, you're the orchestra. The rest of you will be the chorus, and I will lead the music. Line up, everybody!"

Heroes, let your voices ring.
To our island home we sing.
Shelter us from stormy seas.
Keep our kitchens stuffed with cheese.
Save our pelts from lice and fleas.
Save our pelts from fleas and lice.
Shout it once! Shout it twice!
Friends forever! Skog and mice!